In Your Backpack

Dona Herweck Rice

Publishing Credits

Rachelle Cracchiolo, M.S.Ed., *Publisher*
Conni Medina, M.A.Ed., *Managing Editor*
Nika Fabienke, Ed.D., *Content Director*
Véronique Bos, *Creative Director*
Shaun N. Bernadou, *Art Director*
Carol Huey-Gatewood, M.A.Ed., *Editor*
Valerie Morales, *Associate Editor*
Courtney Roberson, *Senior Graphic Designer*

Image Credits: All images from iStock and/or Shutterstock.

Teacher Created Materials
5301 Oceanus Drive
Huntington Beach, CA 92649-1030
www.tcmpub.com

ISBN 978-1-4938-9824-4

Printed by: 590835
Printed in: China

a  for you

pencil

a  for you

paper

a  for you

book

a  for you

bookmark

a  for you

crayon

a  for you

drawing

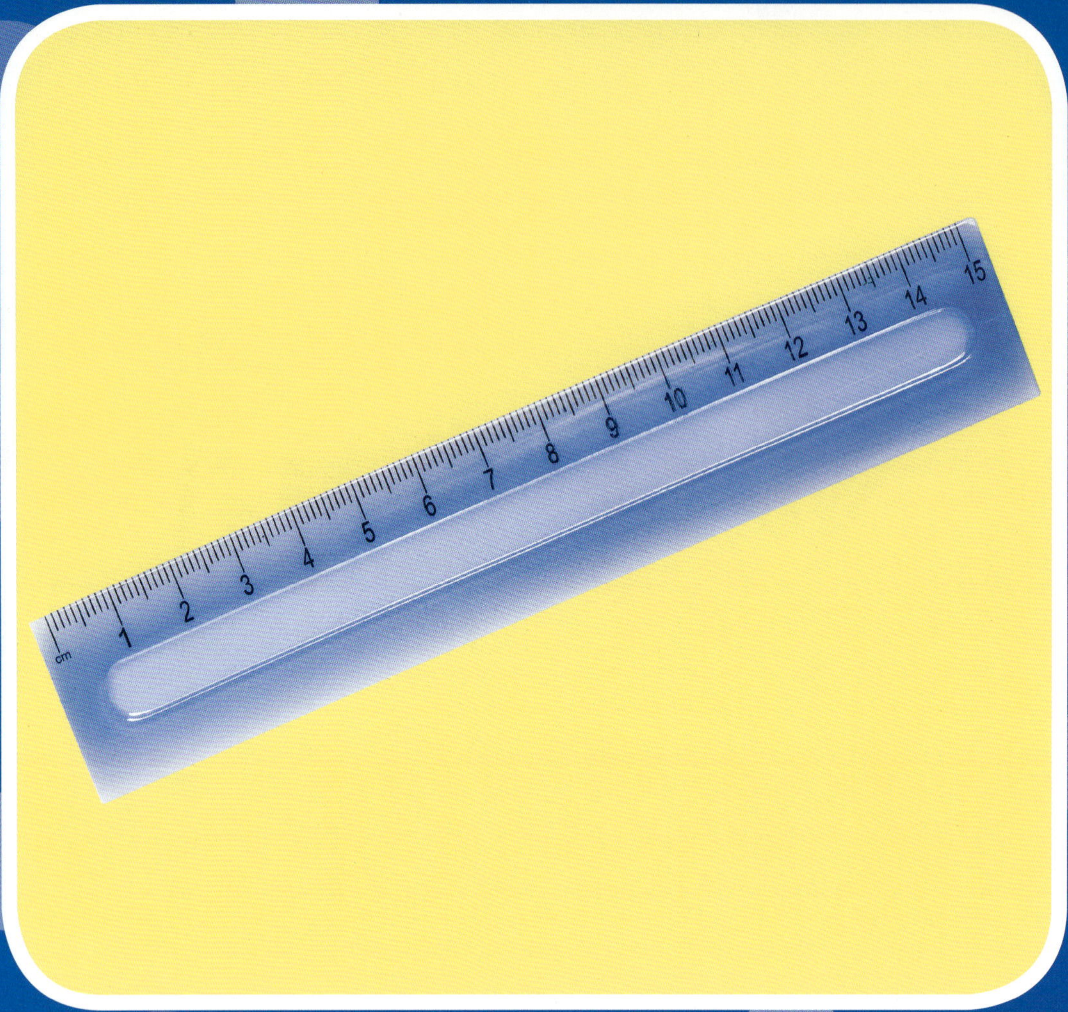

a  for you

ruler

a  for you

glue stick

a  for you

lunchbox

a  for you

water bottle

High-Frequency Words

a

for

you